Finding Love In Fifth Cross

RAHUL RAMESH

RIGI PUBLICATION

Finding Love In Fifth Cross
RAHUL RAMESH

Originally published in the India

ISBN: 978-81-921311-4-6

Published by RIGI PUBLICATION
777, Street no.9, Krishna Nagar
Khanna-141401 (Punjab), India
Website: www.rigipublication.com
Email: info@rigipublication.com
Phone: +91-9357710014, +91-9465468291

Printed at Aarna Printing Solutions, Patiala

Dedicated to Dad.

Late Sri M.K. Ramesh

We miss you.

Acknowledgements

They say that writing is one man's job. They say it wrong. Every sentence in my novel came out of mind because of the support I had.

I am thankful to my mom, P.K. Jayashree and sister Sharada.R for being the best family and supporting me to fullest.

When it comes to friends, they guided me the best way. I thank all my friends for the support.

I should be thankful to Umesh Sehgal, CEO, Rigi Publication for having belief in my work.

I should be thankful to Mr. Benny.K.G for being the backbone of the vocabulary of the novel.

Chapter-1

The Way It Started

If you were in Navanagar 5th cross bus stand around 8 in the morning of a weekday, a couple of years ago, you would have seen two guys.

Rajan was the guy who was short and handsome to look, he was my roommate and we were of the same college and department. Our department was Electronics and Communication. The other was me, a teenager who was tall with long funky hairstyle with spectacles.

We both shared a room in fifth cross of Navanagar. It is an area in Banpur. The city, Banpur is well known and even vast.

We were in the final year of our course of three years. We both were single until that day when he proposed a girl, who he used to stare everyday in fifth cross bus stop since a year at that time.

He used to stare that girl in bus stop, in bus and even after she getting down from the bus until she is totally out of sight. That girl was our neighbour, she was doing her +1(first year PUC) in a college which was just few kilometres away from 5th cross bus stop.

Her name is Tanya. We had our room on the first floor. The pale yellow building, which used to glow a little in the morning and which was next to our brown building was Tanya's house.

Rajan's gaze was not one way; even she used to look him intently many a time. They had their own world in that exchange of looks; it was easy to see Rajan and Tanya in their respective terraces each evening and Sunday was an exception as they used to be in the terrace the whole day.

My friend used to have his text books with him and used to study in the terrace, she used to come to the terrace with her book every day, sometimes I have seen economics text, sometimes business studies, accounts and sometimes computer science in her hand and it proved that she was a commerce student.

It was a pretty love story which never had anything more than stares and gazes for a long time nearly around a year. In that whole year I never heard her name in his voice.

Even if they used to exchange that intent looks for the whole year, they never got a chance to talk as Tanya's father, Mr. Karan Sharma, a black wild looking bald headed man had an eye on both Rajan and me from the day we occupied the room.

That bald man was none other than the younger brother of our landlord. I have never seen those two brothers talking each other. Even the family members of our landlord never had a chat with that family in front of us for those two years as I was staying in the same room from the day one of my course.

Our landlord was the elder one among the Sharmas. Tanya's father was the second one. People used to say there was another one but he left both these Sharmas just after the clash among them.

As per layman's tongue the clash was because of local politics. Our landlord, Manan Sharma was a politician who held his hands high for the past twenty years and was the leader of the party which was fostered by his father. He had a winning streak of continuous four terms.

Karan Sharma was the one who always lost against Manan Sharma in every election that was held in the span of those twenty years and was the leader of the party which he formed twenty years ago.

Coming back to the day when Rajan proposed Tanya. It was a beautiful sunny morning. We both were ready at 7:45. We knew that Tanya's father Mr. Karan Sharma was not at home since a couple of days as we didn't see him.

The bus stop of fifth cross was just a few houses away from Tanya's house. One who stands near the gate of that house could have a perfect vision of the things happening in bus stop and Mr.BB always used to be near the gate when his daughter was in the bus stop. BB was the name given by Rajan to Mr. Karan and the expansion of BB was Bald Black. That name perfectly suited him.

Rajan was waiting for Tanya to leave the house as usual. He used to order me to lock the house and leave soon, just after getting to know that Tanya left her house. I never had a problem with that order. But that day it was not any order it was a question, a question which shocked me for a second.

Anybody in this whole world will call me a fool if I say what that question was but they think in general, my case was different.

Rajan asked me "shall I propose Tanya today? What do you think?" It is the normal question that a guy asks his friend but as said before, Rajan never uttered the name Tanya in front of me and all of a sudden, this question!

After coming out of the shock I replied him that there can't be a better occasion than that. Then he ordered me to leave room as he used to do every day. I locked the room and followed Rajan fast.

Near the stairs we saw Kunal, the only son of our landlord cleaning his bike just like other days to go to his office for his work as he was an engineer.

He smiled at both of us and asked about breakfast. We said that we had and left. We rushed to the bus stop very fast and were very nervous.

She was amidst few people in the bus stop, a bus came and everyone went except Tanya. I knew that she was waiting for Rajan.

I thought it was the luck of Rajan at that moment but never thought it was ill-fated too. I had no guess about the events which were yet to come.

Rajan slowly moved towards her, she was standing in that bus stop alone as there was nothing to sit in that small bus shelter. A year ago it was having an undersized, broken bench but even that wasn't left by the greedy creatures of Banpur.

I never thought that my rich friend had a gift for the one who he loved from a year. He slowly unzipped his bag and gave the gift which was wrapped in red, shining gift wrapper.

By that time I saw Kunal riding his bike very slow as he was busy on a phone call. He saw Rajan and Tanya with that gift in Tanya's hand.

He didn't care a lot and moved. There was no one in the bus stop till that time. I was a bit far from that pair because I thought of giving them privacy.

Both of them were happy. I got to know she accepted by the smiles on her face. Meanwhile I had no other work to do so I was watching here and there.

It was really a nice morning and the weather was still humid and the rays of the sun were making me feel warm. There were a few people in the bus stop then.

The school boy whose house was just next to the bus stop who I used to see getting scolding each and every day by his mom as he was very bad in studies was one among the people in the bus stop.

Next bus came; Rajan and Tanya were not in a mood to leave. Everybody got into that bus including that boy. The bus started to move.

I heard the sound of the gate of that boy's house, which was opened by his mom. Within a fraction of second I saw her on the road. She was running behind that bus. I noticed that she had a lunch box in her hand.

Her age was in mid thirties, she wasn't old but she was having a problem in running as she was wearing a saree, she didn't give up.

I shouted at the driver hoping that he will stop the bus. Driver heard me shout; even he got to know the reason as he saw that lady running behind the bus through the mirrors. The bus gradually stopped.

I saw that mother giving her son the lunch box and she was happy. Her happiness was more than the winner of some running event.

That lady smiled at me and said thanks in a very low tone. Even I smiled and she went back home. Her actions made me think about my mom who was some towns away from Banpur city.

A few drops of tear rolled down my cheeks suddenly. I was missing my mom, her affectionate face, smile and her care. Yes I felt very sad at that moment.

I wiped my cheeks as I never wanted anyone to ask about the reason for my tears in that bus stop. I stood calm for some time and consoled myself.

A few minutes later I went near Rajan and Tanya to say them that it was not safe there to stay for a long time as Tanya's home was not so far.

Even they were scared of Tanya's family but it was the only chance they got to talk after waiting for a whole year.

Their faces were full of happiness until my words, surely the sad expression from them was expected but they agreed to move by the next bus and the events which happened next was beyond imagination.

Chapter-2

Happiness Partially Erases Tension

Tanya kept the gift given by Rajan in her college bag. She was happy, even my rich friend too. No words can explain that gladness, it was just amazing to see their faces at that moment. They were planning for the next meet but that couldn't happen as the next bus came.

He gave her a goodbye smile and we slowly moved towards the backdoor of that Banpur City Transport Corporation (BCTC) bus. Front door is for ladies and sometimes even gents also use it. Rajan got into the bus. I was about to get in and I saw BB getting down from the front door and I was sure that he saw Rajan and Tanya together.

BB started to talk with Tanya; I was able to see Tanya's face but was not able to see his face as their faces were facing each other. She was talking to her father with a smile on her face but that fear was flawlessly visible. She was the last to aboard the bus from front door and I was the last in back door.

Rajan did not know the event which I saw as he was in the middle of some people in that jam-packed bus. There was a distance between Rajan and me as the bus was crowded. It didn't take much time for me to be near him.

I told him the scene of BB which I witnessed a few seconds ago. He asked about the expression of BB and the reaction of Tanya and I could only say that she was talking with a smile on her face as I was able to see only Tanya's face but not the face of Mr Karan Sharma. Some people were hearing my words but I didn't care as saying that to Rajan was more important to me at that time.

He tried to locate Tanya in that bus; he couldn't find her as the bus was packed. He tried every possible way to find her and it was not possible, even a tall boy like me was unable to find her as that bus was much crowded. In each and every stop, the people who got in were more than the people who got down and that made the possibilities of finding Tanya more difficult.

People in the bus were looking us in awkward way as if they never tried to search someone in the bus in their whole life.

Within no time the bus was in Tanya's stop and Rajan saw her getting down. She was searching for Rajan; she was having a tensed smile on her face.

The bus started moving and she saw him finally through the blurred window of that bus, even in that tension she was smiling and she waved at him. She was totally out of sight even before his hands stopped waving.

He was unable to speak anything. He was nervous but happiness was more than that. Moreover he talked with Tanya after a long wait of one year. Yes, he got to know that BB saw them but that tension was erased partially by the happiness of the chat he had with Tanya.

I asked him about Tanya and he said that she accepted and he started to say the conversation of him with Tanya to me. His happiness made me to forget what I saw when I was about to get into the bus. He was saying about his conversation with Tanya.

His words were showing his love towards her, without my attention we were near our college stop. He was still saying about that conversation itself.

I was too curious about that story, There was nothing extra ordinary in that but hearing from a heart which waited for a year for this moment was awesome.

By that time we were near our college as the college was not too far from the bus stop. He was saying everything in total excitement until the lecture started.

He was a very curious student and it was rare to see him talk with other students when the lecturer was inside the class room.

I was not interested in the class as usual and called Rajan to accompany me to bunk the remaining classes even if I knew that his reply will be in negation and as expected he said "I will not bunk, I have interest in the lecture."

As a matter of fact I was a fool to ask a guy to accompany me to bunk the class who had cent percent attendance in previous semesters.

I came out of the class and I saw Punith playing cricket with his branch mates. Punith was a student in civil department, he was of my type, we loved music a lot and we used to write lyrics of our own. I was interested in rapping, he used to like singing. As our passion was similar we both formed a vocal band called vocal symphony.

I waited for that match to end and called Punith to the room to do a song, we went to our room to create a new song for our band.

We reached our room and searched the best lyrics amongst the ones we wrote. We got the perfect one and we checked for the instrumentals we had and we selected one among them.

We practiced the lyrics with the music for some minutes and then we started recording. We were not having a perfect studio to record. We were not that rich to afford a studio. All we had was my laptop, common recording software and a normal microphone. We continued doing songs in this manner. All we had in mind was to let people know about the songs. That particular day we completed just a part of a song taking few hours.

It was nearly 4 pm in the clock and that was the time for Rajan to return. Punith left, as it was the time for him to go home and I went outside to have some tea.

When I returned back Rajan was waiting for me near the room. He said that he called me and got to know that my cell was in the room when he heard my ringtone coming from the room.

Actually the room was locked from outside and I had the keys. I opened the door and we went inside. He asked me "you saw Tanya today, after coming back?" I replied "no".

He said that he want to see her badly. He was totally tensed. I was preparing coffee for Rajan and myself and I asked him "shall we play carrom outside? So that you can see Tanya as soon as she comes to the terrace". He agreed, I came out of the house with two cups of coffee. He was sitting on the chair in front of a table in which the carrom board was placed.

We started playing carrom and the game was just a reason to be on the terrace for some time, he saw Tanya on her terrace. As usual she had a book in her hand. It was computer science that particular day.

He smiled at her and tried to ask her about the morning's incident with just signs. She was unable to understand his actions so I went inside the room and came with a paper and pen. I told him to write the thing which he wants to ask her and throw towards her.

He wrote "everything okay?" and he threw it. She read that and even she wrote something on it and threw it back. "Ya, there is no problem here, dad did not ask anything" was her reply to Rajan's question. But according to me BB saw them.

I was a bit tired and even wanted to give that pair some precious privacy to exchange their looks and throw paper which was started just a few seconds ago at that time. So I went back to room and slept on the cot.

I was thinking about the day. It was a wonderful experience for me. That day I saw Rajan happier than the day when he topped the university.

Actually he was the university topper for last two years. He couldn't pass mathematics in his second year PUC as he was interested in sports, he was a wonderful basketball player which I got to know by the certificates he had with him.

According to him topping in every semester was the best option to answer those who injured him mentally after his PUC result. He was hard working and I was totally opposite to him.

I used to spend a maximum of two hours to study the subject only on the day before exam as I lived for 35(the minimum marks to pass), two hours were not enough for Rajan every day.

Every lecturer used to scold me and sometimes Rajan for being my friend. Rajan never had problem with others' words, he knew what I was and I knew him totally and that was enough for friendship.

I got to know that I forgot to tell Rajan about Kunal when I was on the cot and even thought that it was not important as according to me every person of our owner's family was least bothered about the members of BB's family.

I was very sleepy but I suddenly heard the message tone of my cell, it was a message of someone special for me in facebook. Actually it was facebook messenger which allowed me to receive messages even when I was not using.

That special person was not special for me just at that time but she is special till now. I used to wait for her to reply to my messages every day. Till today I haven't seen her face to face. The name of that special one is Inchara. According to me she is the most beautiful girl in this world. At that time she just completed her +2(2nd PUC). I was just a boy who used to check facebook always, accept any friend request by any person and used to send some requests of my own.

I was not interested in love at that time as I was chasing success. The destination was clearly visible. Punith and I had same aim.

We were able to see many musicians, singers, rappers and some useless performers on the stage where we wanted to be. I and even Punith always wanted us on that stage, I always dreamt of rapping in front of that massive crowd but nothing was happening just because we were not having enough money to accomplish our dreams.

We have cursed ourselves a lot of time for not being rich by birth. I was not in a mood to love anyone. I just wanted to be successful. I just had my focus on the spotlight.

Three months back to the day when Rajan proposed Tanya, just like other days I sent friend request to this girl and as I used to check Facebook regularly, I got to know that she accepted it the next morning.

She was not online at that time. So I chatted with some friends and logged out. It was two days later from that day, I saw her online. I usually used to send 'hi' followed by my band page link to people.

Becoming famous was my destiny and I used to send my band page link to become famous. It was the only way to start or you can say the only way I had. I sent 'hi' to her first and waited for some time. She didn't reply. After sometime I sent her my band page link. She didn't reply for that also.

She was online for nearly half an hour after that. I was waiting for her to check the songs in the band page. She didn't do it, a like in facebook was very precious for me and even for Punith.

Expecting a like from a stranger to the band page was not really good but we had no choice, I don't know what Punith used to do but I had really sent the band page link to many. Among those many were strangers and some are still strangers and some are so called fans of mine now and even Punith's, some are my friends now and this girl whose dad is a bank manager and whose mom is a housewife and who is the only child to her parents is not like any of those today, she is more than any of those. She is a special one.

I used to see her online each and every day. I was very curious about this girl. Many people never cared for the link that I used to send them and even I never cared about them.

This girl was different. Her profile picture made me see it again and again. I was waiting for her to reply but she didn't do it for weeks.

One day I saw her online and I sent 'hi' again. She did not reply even that time. I poked her and waited for some time. There was no response but I saw that she poked me back the next morning.

I was very happy, I checked whether she was online or not. She was online. I sent 'hi' suddenly and just like previous day, I did not get any reply. I poked her again and then she poked back suddenly.

After few minutes I got to know that she liked my band page. After a short time I received her message "I just listened to your song, its good". It shocked me.

The link was sent few weeks ago and she used to be online every day but it was strange that she took nearly two weeks to check the songs in my band page. I don't know what was special that particular day.

I don't know whether it was special for her or not but it was special for me for sure. If truth to be told, I was waiting for her reply and then started asking about the songs then slowly started asking about her.

She started to chat with me and said about her. She asked about me also, we became a bit close and started to chat every day. She came to know that I used to like her after few weeks.

She stopped messaging me after knowing that I like her. After that I started to send her sorry. I sent it a few times. I was nervous and was waiting for her to reply. She went offline. I was very nervous and was really waiting for her response to that.

I waited for some minutes and I couldn't see her online. I didn't receive a message from her that whole day. The data pack was just for that day so it finished in the midnight and I was not having enough balance to browse without data pack. I couldn't sleep that whole night, it was already 4 in the clock. I was really tensed and was not getting sleep and decided to go out and have some tea.

I was not sure whether I will get tea at that time or not as I have never seen Navanagar then. I was not a boy who used to wake up at 4 even at the exam times. I woke Rajan up and said him to lock room from inside. He asked me the reason in his sleepy mood. I explained him and he locked the door and I started to walk alone on the road.

All I could see was light of those street lights, some tree leaves on the road, fog and some vehicles which were parked near the respective houses.

It was wholly cold, I was factually shivering. Whatever the climate was, it was just able to make changes physically, deep in my heart I was thinking about Inchara alone.

Then I was some footsteps away from the bus stop. I saw a motorbike just near the bus stop, it was not of any resident of that place as it was not parked near any house.

I was looking for the owner of that motorbike and a few seconds later I found him. I saw him with a girl just behind the bus stop. They were kissing each other, his face was familiar to me; he used to come near our college sometimes. I got to know the reason of his coming near our college when I saw the girl's face.

It was real shocker to me as it was Christina, she was of my class. She was a brilliant student and even she was living in a separate room with her friends, it was somewhere near Navanagar 1st cross. She was the second topper for our class and was one of the favourites of lecturers.

I never thought that she was a girl behind a bus stop, kissing a guy at 4 in the morning. Even if I saw Christina with that guy kissing in that time I never cared about that as I had tension of my own.

I just changed my track of sight and started to move again. I knew that Christina didn't notice me as she was very busy in enjoying that kiss. I never asked Christina anything about this even if I saw her each and every day in class room, I just pretended as if I never saw anything.

I was just in search of a tea stall, just wanted to stay out of that tension and because of the cold weather conditions. My footsteps continued to search a tea stall, after sometime

I was near Banpur City Outdoor Stadium which was in Navanagar itself.

There was a tea stall near the entrance of that stadium, I saw it when I was a few metres away from the entrance of that stadium and started to walk towards the tea stall and many stray dogs started barking.

Five of them tried to attack me, I was conscious and I just took a stone which was on the foot path and made an action of throwing it. Three dogs ran away and two became more violent. I had no option other than throwing it. I threw towards that black dog, it would have hurt the dog a bit but according to me it was the only way to get rid of those ridiculous violent dogs. I was totally free of dog attacks and went to that tea stall, some of them were still barking but none had the guts to come near the tea shop.

I just ordered the tea and sat on the plastic stool. I was trying to enjoy every sip of the tea but those dogs didn't allow me to enjoy fully. I started to hate those dogs as they were still barking. Those dogs were totally out of my sight as the tea stall and the owner of it blocked my view.

A few minutes later the bark of those dogs stopped and it was beyond my belief so I stood up to see where the dogs went. Those two violent dogs which I saw before were not there this time. I saw some other dogs and they were approaching the tea stall. I kept my tea down on the floor of the stall and ran out to take a stone as according to me these dogs didn't allow me to enjoy my tea when I was tensed and when it was very cold. My intention was to hit those dogs with a stone and to hurt them. In a fraction of a second I was in the footpath and took a stone.

I was about to throw it but suddenly I felt warmth on my shoulder. It was the hand of an old man. Maybe he was in his late fifties or early sixties.

"What are you doing" he asked. "You don't know uncle these dogs spoiled my mood today. I won't leave them" I said. He just smiled and said "I think those were not the dogs which spoiled your mood, they may be these two" pointing to the dogs which were standing just behind him. It was a surprise for me, the two dogs which were totally violent made no noise and seemed innocent for me at that time.

I asked "how do you know"? "Ah. These dogs are my family from the day when my son left me and went to abroad thinking that money is precious than dad" he said, "he visits me once in a leap year and calls me once in six months." He continued in a sad voice and keeping slow steps towards that tea stall, even I followed him.

Then the owner of the tea stall had some biscuit packets in his hand and he handed it to that old man. I took that unfinished tea cup which was left on the floor and started to drink tea again. That old man opened all the biscuit packets and kept the biscuits on the footpath. Within no time the dogs finished eating all those biscuits. Then he came near the stall again, the owner of the stall had some bun in his hand and he handed it to the old man again. All dogs got a bun each and they were just standing near him after eating it.

He came to the tea stall again and took the tea glass which was kept on the owners table. He started to drink tea and asked about me with his low dilapidated voice.

I introduced myself to him and he introduced himself as Naseer. He was a Muslim by birth and had a lot of respect for his religion and all living beings except his son. I got to know all these by his words and got to know that he comes exactly at 4:30 every morning to feed those stray dogs.

The dogs which once irritated me a few seconds ago, made me feel comfortable and their faces which once looked arrogant was just looking innocent at that time. When I started to ask about him, he explained me that after the death of his wife, his family is just these dogs and literally there were some drops of tear in my eyes.

He was not feeling bad as he took life in an enthusiastic way. Even if his feelings had pain in them, he explained it in a funny manner and that was one of the most impossible lesson to learn in one's life and he was an expert in that.

He spends nearly 50 Indian rupees for those dogs each day. This shows the difference between him and his son. Even if they had same blood flowing in their body, father spends money for stray dogs each day and son leaves his old father alone in home for money and takes a plane to abroad.

My tea cup was empty at that time and even his tea cup was. I was not willing to move from that place, without much conversation he just attracted me and we had no other choice than leaving that place.

He gave me a goodbye smile and I responded to it, he went to his home and I started walking towards my room. No other shop was open at that time so I couldn't recharge my cell with internet pack. I just had to wait for a couple of hours for shops to open.

I reached the room, knocked from outside, Rajan opened it and went to the cot to sleep again and I sat on the plastic chair.

I was in need of internet pack and wanted to see whether she replied or not. I wanted to know what she really thinks about me but to my luck I was not having data pack that particular day.

Somehow those two hours passed and it was 6:30 in the clock. It was the time when I used to wake up every day and I knew that the general store next to the apartment on the left of our house will be open.

They used to recharge for all cell phone networks. I just left my room and went directly to the store to recharge my cell phone. The shop was open and I recharged my cell phone with an amount suitable for internet data plan.

It takes nearly half an hour for the activation of the data plan even after the recharge. That half an hour was one of the most frustrating half an hours of my life.

Somehow the data pack activated after half an hour and I opened facebook as soon as possible, if she had sent me a message I would have received it with the help of messenger even if I do not open facebook.

I forgot about messenger in that tension and simply opened facebook. There was no message from anyone. I sent her sorry again. Some days passed and I was waiting for her message.

She didn't text me but I got to know that she was not using facebook as I was checking her page each and every day. She used to like or comment in some or the other post each and every day but that didn't happen for nearly a month or more.

I never saw her online on those days. One fine evening I just received her message in facebook. That was the evening of the same day when Rajan proposed Tanya. She asked sorry for not messaging me these days and even explained the reason. That reason shocked me.

Her message was "sorry for not messaging you all these days, I couldn't reply as I was in hospital. I liked you from the day you started to chat with me and started to like you more and more as days passed but never had that courage to say you as I was never sure of my life. I was a heart patient till that day when I messaged you last, my operation was just the next day. Now I am totally fine, Doctor told that I will be discharged after a month, I couldn't wait for a month to text you so I texted you as soon as possible. I am really sorry."

I started to love her more than I used to do and even texted the same to her. She replied that she loves me too. She asked my number, I gave her and she called me within no time.

I heard her voice for the first time, it was awesome. It was as sweet as honey. Her first hello still echoes in my mind. I will never forget that hello. We started to talk and she asked me "won't you feel like asking about the heart problem I had?" I replied no as I had decided not to ask anything about her past and was just to show love and care as much as possible in present and future.

I told her these things she just cried a bit even I shed tears because of happiness but I just wiped it and consoled her and started to say about Rajan and Tanya's love story to her.

It's funny to say that Inchara argues with me always that Rajan and Tanya's story is better than us but according to me ours will always be the best. She had been the one who always helped me to be tensionless. In tough times she boosted me up mentally and was always there for me. We started to talk on phone regularly but only when she called me because she had told me not to call at all. Every day I used to wait for her call even if I had a long chat with her the previous day. Our loved ones, their smile, talks and their care faded the tension of BB partially.

Chapter 3

The Most Unexpected Thing

Some days passed with a lot of happiness and I used to talk with Inchara each and every day. Rajan used to look Tanya and even she used to look at him many times a day. Rajan told me that he met her two more times near her college after that day.

Our life was good until that day when the most unexpected thing happened. It was our college fest that day; I was totally ready with jeans, t-shirt and a leather jacket and was wearing stylish sunglasses. Rajan also was looking awesome in a cool casual dress.

It was a sunny morning when we left our room to college. It was 7:45 on the clock as usual. Just like other days, we met Kunal near the stairs, he smiled at us and we also gave a smile and started to move, BB was standing near the gate of his building as you might expect.

Tanya was clearly visible in that bus stop as there was no one in the bus stop that day. But to our surprise even she was not having any college bag with her that day. She was wearing a pink top and skirt in which she was looking pretty. Those high heels were adding beauty to her.

We were in the bus stop within no time. I saw that small kid whose father was carpenter and who used to work in the furniture shop which was just next to the hotel and was opposite to the bus stop.

Every day that carpenter used to bring his child with him to work. That kid always used to ask his father to buy him a fish and a fish bowl.

As the aquarium shop was just next to the hotel, that kid always used to ask his father to buy a fish. I never saw him scolding that kid even if he was not having enough money to buy that kid a fish and a fish bowl. The carpenter always said his child "this stock is not good, I have said them to bring good fish to buy you one" and never said him that he is not rich enough to buy one. He would have cursed himself a lot of times for not having enough money to buy his four year old boy a fish and a fish bowl.

On that particular day father and the son were inside the aquarium stall and the father was paying money for the fish and the fish bowl which his son had in his hand.

The eyes of that four year kid were glowing. That fish was everything for that kid, it was his dream from three to four months by that time and even the eyes of the carpenter shone with happiness. Finally after some months he was able to buy a fish and fish bowl to his son.

Maybe that was one of the happiest moments for both the carpenter and his son. Even I was happy by seeing that carpenter and his son.

Rajan was just looking at her; he was unable to talk with her as BB was watching us. A bus came and we all got into it. He went near Tanya as soon as we got into the bus as it was not that much packed that day. They were talking a bit and she got down in the same stop as she used to get down every day.

He came back to me and said "she was not having college today but just lied to her parents that she had some official work in the college office just to see me". He said that he called her to our college function and she rejected as the children of her father's friend were studying in our college itself.

I asked him why he hadn't gone with her. He said that he was not in a mood to miss my performance with Punith in the fest and he was having a prize for the best academic student as he was the topper of the university. I just said thanks to him but inside I was very happy. Even I felt bad that she would be alone and said the same to him. He said "she is going back to her home after 15 or 20 minutes and she was not sad when I said her that I can't go with her today as I said the reason".

We went to college and met our other classmates. I went with Punith to practice for our performance and Rajan was sitting with our branch guys.

Time to start the program was 10am according to the schedule. It started exactly at quarter past eleven because of some reasons.

According to the schedule cultural programmes were after the prize distribution. Punith and I had won some prizes in sports and cultural events. We were happy when Rajan received the award. This was the fourth award for him in the same category as he was the topper of the university for all four semesters. Punith and I found him happy when we were receiving our awards.

The award function got over exactly at 4:45pm and it was having a lot of unnecessary lectures. Rajan was hearing each and every word of the guests. Punith, me and some other guys were just laughing at each and every word of them.

We were missing one of our best friends Jaffar as he was out of station. It was a great experience as all those guests were tremendously funny.

After 4:45 our principal Mr. Vinayak Godse announced that all students should have their snacks before the cultural programme, food committee members are distributing the snacks near the mechanical department lab. Everyone should follow queue and should be back within half an hour.

Mr Godse was a very strict man; he was perfect to his designation. We had snacks which was pretty refreshing. The cultural programmes started and our programme was the third one according to the schedule.

First two programmes were not that much interesting. People were waiting for our song to come as Punith and I were well known for singing. Rajan was not having interest in any other programmes but was waiting for our performance. One of the anchors called our name and the crowd was cheering totally.

They had a lot of expectations on us and we were good enough to satisfy their expectations.

Each and every one enjoyed our song to the fullest. That five and half minute performance totally thrilled them. After the completion of the song we came back to Rajan, while coming back many people said that they really enjoyed the performance.

Rajan had no interest in any other programme as he knew that no other performance will be as good as mine and Punith's. After saying that our performance was awesome he said that he was going back to the room.

We knew that he was about to say the same thing as we have seen him in a lot of college programmes. We went to the tea stall together to have some tea before he left.

We had tea and said that we would accompany him till the bus comes. He refused that as he knew that we wanted to enjoy the programme, as we were programme freaks.

It was half past six, we said him bye and came back to the college premises to watch the programme. We danced like mad people for each and every song nearly a group of 7 people were dancing with us totally behind that crowd.

We enjoyed to the fullest, more than one third of the crowd were watching our dance rather than watching the dance on the stage, we extremely enjoyed each and every programme. We did not know the time till the end of the function; it was 10:30pm when all people were going back to their homes and many students too.

Some ten guys stayed there for some more time to pile up the chairs, remove the connections of computer to the loud speaker and to keep that computer and speaker in the computer lab. I was one among those ten.

It was not a big deal for us to do this work; we finished it fast as we could as we had the experience of six functions. It took half an hour to complete that work which was given to us by our principal.

After that, those who stayed in hostel went to their hostel, the day scholars to their homes and I went back to my room.

The room was locked from outside, I thought Rajan went to the hotel to have food as he usually used to have food in that hotel which was next to the aquarium shop and opposite to the 5th cross bus stop.

He used to have food in that hotel when both of us had no interest to cook on our own. Without further thinking and even without calling to his number, I went to that hotel as I thought I would find Rajan there and even I was very hungry too.

That hotel was not so big. It was very easy to find people in that hotel as there used to be only few many a time. After entering the hotel I looked each side of that small hotel but Rajan was not visible anywhere.

I called to his cell phone but it was busy. I was tensed but was very hungry and thought that Rajan will be in the room when I go back after finishing my dinner.

I had my dinner in that hotel and while having dinner I called Rajan's number it was busy still. I was unable to talk to him as it was busy for next half an hour. I went back to the room and was waiting for him to come, it was just an hour short to midnight and I was really tensed. I was trying to call him many times and heard busy tone each time I tried.

A few minutes later I got a call from Rajan's number and I suddenly picked it and shouted "where are you?" when I heard the reply from the other end it shocked me a bit. It was not Rajan who was on the other side; it was his mom, Sulekha aunty, who was a business lady. She had a well established company which was perfectly established by her husband and she was helping her husband in business all the time. Rajan's father, Mr. Suman Tiwari was a well known business man. He was always busy and couldn't manage his business all alone and his wife was always there for him to help.

I did not know the reason for her voice in Rajan's cell phone all of a sudden until she said me, actually she didn't tell me the whole thing but I had a clue about the situation by the tone of her voice. She said me "Come to Navajyoti Hospital as soon as possible" and cut the call. Navajyoti was a multi speciality hospital which was near the Stadium.

I had guess of the thing which took place but did not know what happened exactly. I was there in Navajyoti within few minutes as it was not too far from our room. My guess was right but not fully, I knew that there was something wrong with Rajan but never thought that it will be severe.

Rajan's mother came and hugged me, actually she used to treat me like her other son even Rajan's father was very close to me, she was unable to speak also. I witnessed a totally bold lady who I used to see ordering others, crying with pain.

I consoled her and went to Rajan's father to know what actually happened to Rajan as I did not know anything and as aunty was unable say anything. I couldn't believe my ears as I heard that Rajan was unconscious. I rushed to the ward to see Rajan and saw a police man and a doctor talking to each other. Rajan was lying on the bed of that special ward.

According to the doctor it was not at all an accident and it was an attack on him from somebody. I went near Rajan and that police came near me and said "are you the one who stays with this boy?" "Yes" I replied and he said Tiwari uncle to meet him in the police station the next morning as it was around 1 am in the clock and even said that I should be with Tiwari uncle during interrogation.

It was some auto driver who took Rajan to the nearby hospital when he found him injured in the outskirts of

Banpur. The auto driver also called his mom and informed her as he found her number in Rajan's cell phone.

After the arrival of aunty to that hospital, Rajan was shifted to Navajyoti from that hospital as it was lacking facilities and as Rajan was very much serious.

Doctor said that he will regain consciousness after some six or eight hours and he will totally be okay and there was nothing to worry much as there was no extreme damage to the nerves of his head. His head was covered by bandages. His right arm was fractured and each and everywhere there was a wound.

Uncle was talking with that police and the doctor just outside the ward and aunty was there inside the ward. She was still crying and even I had tears in my eyes but controlled it as my job was to console her and not to cry and make her cry more.

It was the next morning and some of Rajan's relatives came to the hospital to see him. I was sitting on a stool to the right of Rajan. That day I got to know how miserable thoughts a human can get. It was Rajan's grandmother, Sulekha aunt's mother and she knew everything about the situation, that Rajan was attacked by someone and that he was unconscious at that time. She came and hugged Sulekha aunty and when she came near Rajan she told, "Oh this was the dress I gifted him on his birth day but now this dress is of no use," as if she cared only for the dress. Hearing those words I was just amazed and was thinking that a lady who has nearly 60 years of her life experience on this earth can think only like this. It was the most frustrating dialogue I have ever heard in my life and I thought that someone would say that it was not the time to talk of dress but it didn't happen that way, instead Sulekha aunt's younger sister told that old lady, "Yes I too remember that, he was very happy with your gift and I think you took it in the shop which I showed you right?" "Yes it's a very good shop for clothes," the miserable old lady replied. They were here to see Rajan who was unconscious but they started to talk about clothing. It's really of no use of going to a place if we don't react to the way we should.

We did not know about the one who did this to Rajan. A couple of hours passed and Rajan was still unconscious and I had a doubt on BB but I didn't say anything as I was not having confirmation of that.

Tiwari uncle called me outside and I followed him, he asked about Rajan's enemies but Rajan was not having any enemy, he was friendly with each and everyone. So I said that there was no enemy for him and he gave me the keys of the room which was there in Rajan's pocket. It was given to him by the doctor and told me to be ready in an hour, to go to police station. I just nodded to his words and went back to the ward.

I was having a doubt on Mr. Karan Sharma but I didn't tell as I thought that revealing Tanya's matter was not good at that point of time. I didn't go to the room as I had called Punith and some other friends and informed them about this. I called one of my best friends Jaffar and he said "I will be in Banpur as soon as possible". They were about to come so I thought of going to the room after meeting those guys.

Everybody came as fast as possible and these young lads were more sensible than Rajan's so called grandma. They all visited the ward and maintained silence for some minutes as they were not in mood to hurt Rajan's mother who was just beside Rajan.

When they went out of the ward I went to talk to them. As soon as my right leg crossed the door of the ward Punith hugged me and started to cry. I knew what he was feeling but I felt more than him but I couldn't express that as I knew that it would hurt Sulekha aunt more

This time there was no aunty by my side, we were not in her view also, even if I was trying to control myself, I couldn't. Tears rolled down my cheek within no time, other friends consoled us and all of them went to their home after few minutes and I went to the room. I haven't had a sleep for that day; I was tired and was unable to sleep also. I was on the road and was walking to the room as it was not too far from the hospital, there were many people on the road but I was feeling lonely.

Then I was near fifth cross bus stop, it was looking something unusual to me as I was alone that day and just wanted to kill time but it was not happening. Minutes were like hours and hours were like days to me without Rajan.

I went to the room, took bath after heating the water using the electric geyser. That bath refreshed me physically but was not enough to kill the sadness in my mind. I dressed up myself and sat on the cot, waiting for uncle.

I did not know about the culprit but had a lot of doubt on BB.

It was just some minutes away to be in the police station, answering their questions and I was just thinking whether I should say about BB or not? I knew that we should not blame anyone until we have confirmation and I learnt this from the story which was told my grandfather and this story really helped me to take good decisions.

Just look at your problems and just look at your past. There will be something which may help you to come out of your problem. It may be the movie which you saw when you were 15 or it may be the moral story which you read when you were 8. In this case I found a story.

Chapter 4

The Story Which Helped Me

You may not believe my words but it was a story which helped to get an answer to my own question "whether I should say about BB or not?" This story was told to me by my grandfather years ago, maybe when I was 8 or 9 years old.

I felt that this is one of the worst stories I have ever heard as I was not too old to understand it wholly at that time and this is not a story of superman or bat man who has extraordinary powers to entertain an 8 or 9 year old boy, but now when I look at the list of the stories I heard at that age which is somewhat full of heroic characters, this story stands tall. This story is of a Brahmin priest and the forest of ten robbers.

"There lived a Brahmin priest in a village which was just next to a huge forest. On the other side of that forest there was another village, people once used to go to that village using the forest trail but it has been years since the forest trail was used and people started to use the mud road which was really a long route to that village. There was a reason to use the mud road instead of that forest and the reason was those ten robbers.

It has been seen that only one in that recent past has come alive from that forest. He was the one who gave information of those ten robbers. He was alive because there were a lot of humans who were walking with him in the forest and when those robbers attacked, he ran away and they did not concentrate on him as others were still on their hold.

This Brahmin priest who was famous for doing rituals in both villages had a wish; it was to reach the other village by walking on the forest trail. The distance of both the villages was not walk able even if they walk in forest also. It takes a normal man 12 hours to reach the other village. There was no other village nearby so even if it was 12 hour journey by walk they used to go to that village. If it was using the road, it was nearly a day or even more. If it was in cart then it would have taken some twelve hours but everyone wasn't rich to own a cart. They had enough strength in their legs to walk miles and miles.

This young priest was having no work on the other village at that time but just wanted to go there by walking on the forest trail.

It was a fine evening when he decided to leave to that village the next morning, before people start walking on his village. He planned for his walk and made some food to eat during the journey. He didn't sleep whole night and as he never wanted to get late and never wanted any other to see him walking towards the forest because he knew that they will stop him.

He knew that there are people who will be awake just before the sun rises and he decided to leave very fast. He left his home and was near the forest in half an hour as it was a bit far from his home.

He had three bags with him, one was small and it had some food in it and the other was comparatively large and it had some items of his daily rituals and the largest one was having some fruits and some gold coins as gold coins was the currency those days. On the way he saw nobody and he was happy that he was going to enter the forest today.

It was the dream which he had from many years and was never able to see what was there in the forest. He was afraid of the robbers but also thought that it may be rumours.

He wanted to check it was real or not and he even wanted to see the forest as he heard from his father that the trees in the forest is beautiful, fruits are tasty and the fragrance of the flowers is the best part of that forest. The Brahmin knew that fragrance was the best part of the forest as the smell of the forest attracted him a lot of times when he was walking near the forest. One could smell that fragrance even if he is not inside the forest.

Fragrance was the main reason for him to get attracted towards the forest and he just wanted to enjoy that fragrance fully by going to the forest. His dream of years was just in front of him and he was just short of some steps to initiate it. He was afraid of those ten men but had made in his mind to continue even if he had fear as it was his dream to enter the forest.

Without thinking much, he entered the forest and started walk on the trail which was partially visible because there was no one to step on it and keep it clear. There haven't been human steps on that trail for years and those who dared to step on that trail never came back. He was in heaven of fragrance and it was dream come true for him and he was very happy for initial couple of hours. The sun had risen by that time and he saw a small pond.

He thought of taking bath there and even thought of doing his morning rituals as it was the perfect time to do that. He kept all those bags below a tree which was some distance away from the pond and went to the pond to take bath. While going to the pond he saw a human skull and some bones and it scared him but he continued to walk towards pond.

That skull and those bones made him to think about the ten robbers and even made him to worry about his own life. He was in a dilemma the two things which were in his mind, to go back or to continue and his decision was finalised just before finishing his bath. He decided to continue and decided not to leave no matter what happens.

After his bath he started to walk towards that tree where he kept his bags. Even while going back he saw those bones and that skull. It scared him again but he was firm with his decision to continue that journey. When he reached the tree he saw the place where he kept his bags and saw only two bags. The bag which he found missing was the one which had gold coins in it.

It was not missing as he found it in the hand of a man who was some feet away from that Brahmin. That man was dark in complexion and was having a long, thick beard. His dress was not at all natural as he wearing a cloth around his waist and there were weapons which were tied to a small rope. That rope was also around his waist. Yes he was one of the robbers who people were talking about. That Brahmin just saw the robbers face once, didn't see it again as he was afraid.

He just wanted to stay alive and wanted to be away from that robber. He did not know what to do. He took the bag in which there were some ingredients of the daily rituals and he took those things and started his daily rituals. The man, who was doing it with lot of concentration from the day he started, was doing it with no concentration. His mind was swinging with some other thought. According to him there was no chance of staying alive as nobody went back home from that forest in those days. He was saying some mantras but was not able to concentrate on it.

He thought that if he delays the ritual; the robber may go and did everything slowly but he saw the robber still standing in front of him. He spent nearly an hour for the work he used to do in twenty minutes every day, still he was not ready to finish it, he was simply killing time. When he saw that robber still in front of him even after an hour, he thought that the robber will not move at all and ended his morning ritual soon. Then he woke up, took his bag and kept the ritual ingredients in it and took the other bag which had some food stuffs in it and started to move.

That robber was following the Brahmin who was walking in snail's pace. Somewhere in the middle the Brahmin stopped and sat down a tree to have his breakfast. That robber had the Brahmin's bag for about couple of hours at that time. That priest was wondering about the silence of the robber but he was not having the guts to ask anything. He kept mum.

He started having his breakfast and that robber was standing just in front of him. Priest was full of fear as he knew that nobody came back after entering the forest in that recent past. He was eating the food slowly and was just killing the time. He thought that the robber will kill him just after he saw that robber, that didn't happen and the robber was with the priest for some time but still didn't show the knife also. That knife was still tied to the rope which was in his waist.

He ate slowly just to kill time and was checking the robber's presence time to time. That robber was just standing in front of the priest without changing position.

Brahmin took a lot of time to finish his food but that robber was still in front of the Brahmin itself. While eating a thought came in his mind, "this robber might be waiting for his other nine friends to kill me." After completing the food he started to walk towards the other village with two of his bags, hands had one each. The other bag was still with that robber who was following the Brahmin. He tried to be as slow as possible just to make a delay to his death. He was not willing to die but had to move as sitting somewhere was not at all an option.

While walking towards the other village, made the mid day rituals just before the noon and took his lunch after some time. The robber was following him for about eight hours at that time and the Brahmin was half way through. He couldn't walk anymore and even wanted to kill time so he planned for a nap.

He slept on the ground where he was getting enough shadow from a huge tree. After resting for an hour he started to walk again. That robber was just sitting beside him and even he started to walk with him. It was the time of sunset when that Brahmin did his evening rituals and he continued his journey.

That journey was just of 12 hours but it was already more than that as he was too slow. It was yet to become night, there was bit sunlight and the forest was not totally dark.

The Brahmin didn't notice that robber having food and thought that robber will enjoy after killing him. When it was totally dark, he saw a light from the other town which factually was the burning flame lamp which was placed outside every village those times. It made sure that he was not too far from the next village. It was nearly an eighteen hour journey and finally he was at the end of the forest.

Just at the end of the forest that robber kept the Brahmin's bag on the ground and started to walk back towards the forest.

Brahmin was shocked and called him back, "won't you kill me? I thought you would do that." "Sorry if I scared you, I would have said it before but I didn't tell as I thought that you understood. I was with you because there are nine others in this forest and they won't hurt you if you are with me." Robber said.

Brahmin, the man who never touched the people of lower cast those times, hugged this robber and said "this was one of the big mistakes I have done, thinking that you are a robber and forgetting that you are a human too, sorry for the thing I thought about you, I know you didn't have food the whole day, here are some fruits which you can use and keep the coins with you. It's a present from me," said he by giving the bag back to the robber. this was the story which was told to me years ago and it helped me to take decision. I had decided not to utter anything about BB without confirmation.

Chapter 5

The Interrogation

I was totally ready and Tiwari uncle picked me to Navanagar police station in his car. In the police station the police officer started asking about Rajan to uncle and me. Uncle said that Rajan was not at all a boy of fights and he loved studies and was the topper in the university for four continuous semesters. My words were also almost the same.

The police officer was just trying to ask us about his enemies but the answer was the same. He asked me when I saw him before that incidence and I clearly explained him everything. He said that he would file that case and produce it to the court within 24 hours. Tiwari uncle said, "It's better to know what really happened and then register the case, Rajan will be alright in some hours by now, maybe one or two, and his words will help you more to crack the nut".

The police officer agreed to his words and said, "Yes its better if we register the case after his words because he is the only one who knows exactly about the event".

After all those talk with the police officer in front of me, uncle told me to be near the car and wait for him. I knew that he is about to talk something more but I couldn't stay there as he told me to be outside.

While going out, I received a call from Jaffar and he said that he just had gone to the hospital and saw Rajan there. He said that he wanted to see me and would come to the park which was just a few minutes walk from our college. He said that he would be in the park in half an hour and I said that I also would be there by the same time.

I went back to uncle and told him that I was going to meet a friend and he agreed to that. There was no city bus from Navanagar police station to our college. It was not that far as it had a shortcut. I took an auto to that park and was there in that park within fifteen minutes.

I was waiting for Jaffar; I got a call from Inchara and was talking to my love to spend time as I knew that Jaffar will be late. While talking I was just walking here and there in that park which had huge trees and some flowering plants.

I saw a couple kissing behind a tree and I just didn't care that much at first but when I saw the boy and girl's face it was a shock to me as it was the boy who was with Christina a few weeks back and the girl was not Christina.

I thought it was Christina when I saw his face but got to know later. I never saw him near my college and not even anywhere after that, that was the last time I saw him and Christina didn't act as if she lost her boyfriend. She behaved normally in class everyday and that was more shocking than what I saw in that park.

I was still talking with Inchara and thought that Jaffar would call me so I said her to call me later and cut the call.

After few minutes Jaffar called me and told me to come to the coffee shop which was just opposite to the park and I went there, we had tea and he said that he will not leave the one who did this to Rajan as he was a boy who always used to fight with one or the other in college.

He was very close to me and was best in cracking jokes but it was difficult to stop him when he was in a mood to fight. I said him that police had taken the complaint and will take care of it. Actually he went to a place which was some sixty kilometres away from Banpur as he spent his school days there.

It was the annual day function and he went to that school just to see the girl who he loved from childhood, but he was unable to say his love to that girl as there was no chance of meeting that girl.

He used to call his childhood friends to get her cell phone number but no one gave him. Actually boys were not having her number and girls were not ready to give it as they thought that she will feel bad. Someone close to both of them said him that she would be coming to annual day. So he went there to see her but didn't stay there for much time, actually the time which he spent there was of no use as she was not there in the annual day function when he left. How can she be there if he leaves just after the start of the function?

He said to me that the program was just started when his phone rang and he heard that Rajan was unconscious and he was unable to stay there any longer and just wanted to see Rajan so he came back.

I felt bad when I heard those words from his mouth as I had seen him talking that he is going to meet his love in the annual day function from the day he got to know that she is coming to that annual day.

He told me "we will go back to the hospital now as doctor was saying that Rajan will be conscious in an hour when I went to the hospital"

Chapter 6

Waiting For His Words

Both Jaffar and I went to hospital and we called Punith as we four used to be together always and knew that Punith would be happy if he notices Rajan in a conscious state.

While entering the hospital I saw that old security guard who was past sixty and who was unable to protect the hospital from attacks. I showed him to Jaffar and we laughed at the hospital's owner for keeping him as security and even laughed at that security also. Punith came to the hospital very fast as his house was in Navanagar itself and as he had a two wheeler of his own.

In the ward I saw Sulekha aunty, miserable old lady, aunt's sister, that police man, doctor, nurse and Tiwari uncle. All were waiting for Rajan to talk in curiosity including Jaffar, Punith and me except that miserable old lady who was eating an apple on the corner of that room and started to say "hmm Sulekha, do you remember the taste of the apple I brought to your home a couple of years ago? It was the best apple I have ever tasted and it was 400 rupees per kg at that time I think" she said, aunty was silent and was waiting for Rajan to be conscious again and the old lady continued to talk "even you taste this apple once Sulekha, it is good but not as good as those ones I brought to your home." Aunt became angry and said "my son, your grandson is in the bed of a hospital now, I am waiting for him to talk, I don't want to taste your apple, eat as much as you can and stay silent. We are waiting for him to talk not for your words." That old lady became silent and continued to eat apple.

Doctor was checking Rajan and said Tiwari uncle to buy the prescribed medicines by giving him a sheet of paper which had list of medicines. I suddenly told uncle "I will go, you stay here". He gave me that paper and some money.

I went straight to the medical store which was attached to the hospital and owned by the hospital itself. That medical store was near the main door of the hospital and one could see security guard from that medical store. I gave that shop owner that sheet of paper and was looking at the main door.

I saw that security guard with a small boy. That boy was of 6 or 7 years of age. That old man was sitting on a stool and was holding the hands of that kid who had a cricket bat in his hand.

"He is the grandfather of that child, that child lost his parents in an accident when he was just 3 years of age. Even if his father had some brothers, that old man is the only relationship the kid has as the brothers of his father doesn't care about him. That old man would have sent him to an orphanage but he didn't. Three years ago he came to the hospital in search of a job to take care of that kid. Our owner, the medical superintendent of this hospital gave him that security job even he if he knew that the old man was not physically fit to do it. Both of them stay in a room near the parking lot, that was also was given to them by our owner. Everyone thinks that he doesn't deserve that job but when they get to know about the fact, they will realise that there can't be a better person for the job" said the shop lady who saw me looking at that old man and that child.

This old man deserves total respect.

Actually respect is one of the most misused words in English because if you are a smoker who can smoke ten cigarettes an hour, you will give respect to the one who can smoke twenty an hour likewise a drinker who is capable of drinking five pegs a day will give respect to the one who can drink ten but respect doesn't meant that, it means getting admiration and value from everyone irrespective of their profession or stream. Then I had that plastic cover full of medicines in my hand which was given to me by that shop lady, I gave her the money, took change and went back to the ward.

It was more than given time of eight hours and there were no signs of Rajan's consciousness. The room was silent and the only sound which could be heard was the sound of crip crup from Rajan's grandmother's side as she was eating a pack of chips then. "you know Sulekha" she started to talk again but that words stopped when aunt said " I don't know and I don't want to know, if you want to eat anything else I will get it for you but please, just eat."

'Tanya, Tanya, Tanya.' The words were not clear and not too loud which was uttered by Rajan. Doctor said, "He will be alright from now and there is nothing much to worry as he started talking." There was happiness in every face except that old lady's as the chips she had in her hand was over.

There was something wrong with the expression of the faces. They were happy by the words of the doctor but were confused by the words of Rajan.

Tanya was totally a new word to them, not only for the family members of Rajan but also for Punith and Jaffar as even they were not aware of his love story.

Every face turned towards me, I was looking everyone in a furtive way, I was really trying to avoid myself from that but everyone was just looking at me.

They were approaching me to ask that thing when Rajan said "ma", there was a sigh of relief in me as I heard that sound from his voice and as I knew that everybody would concentrate on him. My guess was right, the track of view of everyone changed suddenly.

They went directly to Rajan, his eyes were open and aunty took his head in her hand, started stroking his hair with her hand. He was looking everybody, old lady was just behind Punith and said "I am unable to see my grandson, you go that way" Punith just moved a bit. He started talking with everyone and after sometime the question rose "who did this to you?" it was Tiwari uncle who asked that.

Police, who was sitting outside the ward a few seconds ago, was inside the ward at that time and he was just next to Tiwari uncle.

Sooner or later we would have had that answer so the doctor said "it's better to ask him after some time as he has just recovered." The police was waiting for his answer. A few minutes later Rajan started to say, "I was not interested in performances so just said them that I would leave" pointing at Punith and me. "We had tea at the bakery and they said they'd accompany me until the arrival of the bus, I rejected their words as I knew that they had interest in the college programmes," with his fingers still pointing us.

"I was alone in the bus stop as all other students were busy with the college function and it was the stop where only college students used to aboard usually. A bike came and there was a guy named Sudesh, I had seen him a lot of times but never had a chat with him, he used to come near our room and I have seen him with Kunal, later I got to know that he was one of the friends of Kunal".

Everyone was listening to him and he was just looking at everybody and used to look at that police more than everyone as he knew that police requires his statement more than anyone.

There were two sounds in the room, one was Rajan's voice and the other was crip crup of the coconut cookies which Rajan's grandmother was eating. "He just came directly to me and he started talking about Tanya after introducing himself as the one who loves Tanya, he said me to leave Tanya as he said he loves her a lot. I told him that I love her more than anyone and she loves me so I can't leave. He just tried to convince but was not able to do it effectively as I loved her more than myself. The conversation ended as I saw the bus of 5th cross. I said him that I would not be leaving her and left the place. I took the bus and went, sat inside as there were only few people," he continued.

"I was out of the bus in some minutes and while I was walking towards the room I got kidnapped. Someone dragged me and I was in a car within no time, I was trying to shout but a hand held my mouth. It was Kunal's. There were two others in that car. I knew that it was because of Tanya's matter but the one who talked to me in our college bus stop was absent there." said Rajan.

Police, "Do you remember those faces? Rajan, "Yes I do." Tiwari uncle said, "It doesn't matter he remembers or not as Kunal is included in the story, we will get information from Kunal himself." Police asked me, "Do you know Kunal?" I said, "Yes, he is the son of our owner." Police further asked me, "Won't you talk with him?" I said, "Not that much, but I thought that he is good." Our conversation ended and we turned towards Rajan to hear his words again.

"It's already 1pm. Can we have our food now? It's better to have food time to time to have a healthy life" The old lady said. Aunty said, "Let's have it later and if you want you can have it in the hospital canteen."

"I was taken to the outskirts of Banpur, they stopped the car and dragged me out. There were no people at that place except me, and those three guys including Kunal. I tried to ask Kunal about the thing but he said me to leave

Tanya before I opened my mouth. I said "I can't" and saw Sudesh coming in his bike at that time. He got down from it and started to talk about the same matter. He told me to leave Tanya but I neglected his words just as before. He slapped me once, I was helpless as I knew that they all would beat me after sometime, I stood silent and broke it later by saying that "I can't leave Tanya, I love her to the core and she loves me too." He slapped me again and I couldn't control myself and punched on his face once. He pushed me and I fell down when I got up to hit him again all the others who were with him started to hit me, within no time they had me in the ground and I tried to escape from them but I couldn't. After some beat downs they stopped and Sudesh warned me again "leave Tanya." I tried to get up and hit him but I was grounded again and this time they hit me more, I don't remember but I know that somebody hit my hand with a steel rod, do not know exactly who did it but someone did it for sure and that's why it is fractured, I don't remember much after that" said Rajan. "It's easy to catch all those guys as you know Kunal" police said looking at me and Tiwari uncle.

Chapter 7

After His Words

After getting to know about the culprits who fractured the hand of Rajan and made him unconscious, the police just said Tiwari uncle and me to be near the room and he would come there to take Kunal.

I was waiting with Tiwari uncle, Jaffar and Punith were there with me as they said they wanted to be with us during the arrest of Kunal and other three guys including Sudesh. Police came in his jeep with two constables he stopped just in front of our building.

The police officer rushed to our owner's house just after getting out of his jeep. Tiwari uncle said me to stand outside and he followed the police officer. They came out after sometime and our owner's wife was just few steps behind them and was asking what the problem was. Police officer said, "You will get to know about it shortly, thanks for giving his office address". He said in his rough voice "follow the jeep and bring those boys with you" he continued and got into the jeep again. We three got into Tiwari uncle's car and he started to follow that police jeep.

Kunal was not at home, he had been to office so the police took his office address to catch him in his office itself. Manan Sharma wouldn't have left the police to arrest Kunal but he was not at home as he had been to a party meeting which was in the party office, the party office was an hour's drive away from his home and the only way for him to release Kunal was to be in the police station as fast as he could.

BB was outside his house, he saw his brother's wife asking the police about the thing which happened but didn't ask anything. Then we were near Kunal's office and the police officer who was out of his jeep came near Tiwari uncle's car and told me to accompany him to bring Kunal out. I joined him, Tiwari uncle and my two friends were waiting outside the office with those two constables.

We were near enquiry by then. Police officer asked the receptionist, "Where can we find Kunal Sharma?" The receptionist replied, "Third cabinet to the right, any problem sir?" Police officer said, "Nothing, thank you". He went straight to that cabin and I saw Kunal sitting there in front of a computer. "Is he Kunal?" police asked me in a low voice, "Yes," I uttered, he grabbed his collar as soon as he heard yes from me. Kunal asked in a furious voice, "What happened, what did I do?" Police officer said, "You will come to know, come with us." Kunal retorted, "you don't know who my father is." Police said, "I don't care who your father is." He took him out of the office holding his collar. Kunal's colleagues were watching him but no one dared to ask about that directly. There was a murmur in the office at that time. Every voice was low and had Kunal in it.

After coming out, the police officer said, "Where are the others?" "Who?" Kunal questioned. The police officer slapped his face and asked "where are the others?" "I don't know, maybe in the place they work" Kunal said. Police officer asked, "All of them are your friends?" Kunal said, "Yes." Police officer asked, "Do you meet frequently?" Kunal said, "Yes".

The police officer said Kunal to call them and tell them to be in the place where they meet regularly. Kunal did it and everyone agreed. "Follow our jeep, let's go to that place and catch them there" police said to Tiwari uncle. Jaffar, Punith, Tiwari uncle and I were in the car which was following that government police jeep.

It was a small hotel which had a bar on the corner. Police officer said to Kunal, "Our jeep will not be visible to anyone, but you can't escape as these three boys, I and the constables will be hiding somewhere" he said in his rough voice, "Take my number, give me a missed call as a confirmation that you have all three of them with you" police gave his cell phone number to Kunal which he noted on his phone. "Don't dare to call your father, you don't know what all I can do to you." The police officer warned Kunal.

Kunal went and sat on a table, police officer ordered us to have an eye on Kunal and the others and not to make a move until all three arrive. "I will call the station and will say some other constables to be here as soon as possible as only two are not enough," police officer said.

All of us were waiting for those three to come. I knew Sudesh as I have seen him with Kunal many times. He was the first to come; the other two came after a few minutes. All of them were talking; Kunal took his phone out of his pocket. I knew that he was about to give a missed call to the police officer. Eventually he did.

Within no time there were some four or five constables around the table in which they all were sitting, Collars of each guy was held by a constable each. We all went there to see what was happening there. Those four guys were asking explanations, the police officer came later and slapped Sudesh, without explaining anything they took them towards the jeep. There were two jeeps, one was the one which we followed in Tiwari uncle's car, the other was the one in which the remaining constables came.

Chapter 8

The Deal

All those constables and those four guys went in police jeeps. Tiwari uncle, Punith, Jaffar and me went in Tiwari uncle's car to the police station. I was surprised to see Mr. Karan Sharma there. I expected Mr. Manan Sharma there, he was not present.

BB was sitting on a chair in front of the main police's desk. The police officer went and sat on his chair. Tiwari uncle sat on the chair which was next to Karan Sharma.

BB was waiting for the police officer to sit and started to talk.

"You know, I never had a chat with the family of my brother from nearly twenty years," he said in a low voice, "still I'm here just because I have taken care of Kunal when he was too little, even if I haven't talked with him from twenty years, I have seen him growing up in front of me. Many here don't know why my brother and me stopped talking, I need to explain it now. We were a good family with love and bliss twenty years ago. My father was the head of the family and was the head of the political party he founded. My father, Manan, Yuvan, Manan's wife, three year old Kunal and me made a great family. That party used to win every election from the day it was founded. Manan and I never had interest in studies, the younger one Yuvan had a lot of interest in academics. Manan had a business of his own, a textile factory. It was well and good until he had profit in his business. I was interested in politics and always had worked for the party when it needed me. Manan's business was under loss when my father expired, he joined the party and we started to fight to become the party leader and the next contestant from that party in our constituency." He took a sip of water from the water bottle which was on the desk. The constables still held their hands on the collars of those four guys. Jaffar, Punith and me were standing behind the chairs of BB and Tiwari uncle.

BB continued to talk after keeping that water bottle on the desk. "According to me I deserved the spot of party leader as I had spent more time with the party than my brother. According to him he deserved that spot as he was elder. The greed to become the party leader was more than the sorrow of our father's death. Manan had more supporters in the party than me, he became the party leader. I left the house and founded a new party. In between all these, Yuvan left the house as he never found care from his greedy brothers. In each and every election I competed against my brother and lost every time. Both me and Manan searched for Yuvan separately but it was of no use. The one who used to be either in college or in house was found nowhere. We were not able to find him since twenty years. I liked Kunal a lot, but I was unable to talk and play with Kunal as I was totally out of touch with their family. Two years after the clash, I married Nidhi, and a year later we were the parents of Tanya. I started my own business, a glass factory and used to compete in every election. After twenty years, it's the first time I'm here for the matter of my brother's family as I like Kunal. I don't want him to be behind the bars. I have lost a brother because of greed, I don't want to see Kunal in jail, so whatever it may take I'm ready to do to see him back in his home without any injury."

He looked at Tiwari uncle and said, "Look, you know that your son is in love with my daughter and nothing will be perfect if I say no, even I want Rajan as my son in law but I don't have any other option. I will agree to their marriage if you say these police to release Kunal."

Tiwari uncle said to the constables, "You release Kunal now, I'll talk with them later." The police officer told looking at a constable, "Leave him". Kunal went to BB without talking much.

"What to do with these three?" asked the police officer. "You know what to do," Tiwari uncle said. The police officer gave a wicked smile and said, "Okay, we will leave them to the spot you told, you show us the way." As a matter of fact, no case was filed against them. Tiwari uncle had a chat with the police officer not to file a case against them when I went to meet Jaffar. Tiwari uncle was rich enough to buy a whole corrupt police station. This corrupt police officer was nothing in front of the money Tiwari uncle had.

That police jeep followed Tiwari uncle's car and it had the police officer in the driver's seat and those three guys were in the jeep with three constables. Somewhat it was packed.

Tiwari uncle was driving the car and asked "Who likes fighting here?" Punith was silent, I didn't open my mouth but Jaffar would always talk when the word 'fight' comes. "I don't like anything else other than that," he said.

"Do you like to hit people?" asked Tiwari uncle. "I always do that near home, even in college and now shall I hit you for driving this much slow?" Jaffar replied. "Then today you will enjoy hitting those three guys in front of the police, you can hit them as much as you want." Uncle said. "I am not mad to hit them in front of police" Jaffar said in a very funny tone. "Don't worry, police will not do anything to you, fifty thousand has its own value" uncle said. "Then I'm ready" said Jaffar. It was already more than forty five minutes drive by that time. We were on the outskirts of Banpur.

Uncle stopped the car in a lonely place which was miles away from the main road. We all got out of the car. The police jeep was stopped just inches away from the rear number plate of uncle's car. The police officer got down and the constables dragged those three guys out of the jeep. Before getting down from the car, uncle told Jaffar to hit them till he is satisfied.

The police warned them not to escape and told them that the consequences will be severe if they try to. They were scared and didn't try to escape. Uncle was in front of those three guys. Just behind uncle was Jaffar. Punith and me were behind him. Constables were standing behind those three guys, Sudesh was in the middle.

"Why did you do this?," uncle asked Sudesh. "I love Tanya" he replied. "So what? She loves Rajan" uncle said in a cool voice. "That's why I tried to move Rajan out of my way" Sudesh said in a high tone. He received a thunderous slap just after finishing his words.

That was not from uncle's hand, It was Jaffar's. That thunderous slap was followed by some heavy blows to the face. He didn't talk, he never used to. Always his hands did. The other two guys were shocked to see Jaffar hitting their friend and tried to stop him, they couldn't as the constables behind them pulled them back. Jaffar was in total action. He never used to spare the one who scolds him or his friend and this guy injured his friend, so he wanted to injure him too.

Sudesh tried to cover his face by his hands but Jaffar was smart enough to hit his chest when he tried to cover his face. We all were simply watching and in no time he turned his face towards one of the remaining two. He started to hit that guy and Sudesh held his hand as he was not controlled by any constable. I didn't know where I had that much anger, I hit Sudesh as soon as he held Jaffar's hand. Punith tried his hand against the remaining one. They were helpless against our angry hands. There were a lot of punches to their faces and hits to their bodies.

Punith and I were not fighting kind of boys but couldn't control our anger at that time. After few minutes, Tiwari uncle told us to stop and we did.

He and the police officer warned the other two guys not to repeat the things and then sent those guys home, their faces were swollen, one's lower lip was bleeding heavily and the other had a broken nose. They ran away from that place as soon as Tiwari uncle told them to leave.

Sudesh, the police and we three guys were left in that place with Tiwari uncle who started to talk looking at Sudesh. "Love is a feeling which should arise and not arisen forcefully, you would have felt it but the same may not happen to the girl" he said, "you had courage to hit a guy even when you knew about further problems which would arise but was not having courage to tell your love to her? This is not the right way to deal with. See now Rajan and Tanya love each other and will marry in future for sure and don't try to peak your nose anywhere"

The police officer slapped Sudesh and told him to leave Banpur and not to come back again.

Tiwari uncle interrupted that police officer's words and said, "There is no need for you to leave the city, you stay here, but don't continue this kind of work. I would have done anything to you, I am rich enough to stay out of the created problems but I am not going to do anything to you. I am a father and I know how your father feel if I do something to you. So you have your life here and you know what I am capable of. So you live your life without doing harm to others.

Sudesh went back to his home and we three guys sat in Tiwari uncle's car and drove towards our room.

Chapter 9

The Discussion

We went back to our room and were waiting for Rajan to come as we got to know that the hospital people are discharging Rajan within an hour. When we were coming back, uncle received a phone from the hospital and was told about the discharge. All of our faces were full of happiness.

Punith, Jaffar, and I stayed in the room, Tiwari uncle went to the hospital.

Maybe after a couple of hours of wait, we saw Rajan's face. He was the first to enter the room, aunt was the next one and she was holding his hand.

"Cucumber is the best to reduce the thirst in summer, but cucumber here is not as good as the cucumber in our place Sulekha," said that old lady who entered next and who had a piece of cucumber in her hand which was partially eaten.

Younger sister of Sulekha aunty was the next and was followed by Tiwari uncle who was keeping the key of his car while entering the room.

Even if the room was of just two guys, it was big enough to hold that much population.

After a few minutes, a miracle happened; Manan Sharma entered the room with BB. I never thought that I would witness that in my life but it happened.

I was not knowing the reason for their presence in the room for some minutes until our owner opened his mouth.

"Twenty long years, we have spent without talking, but today we are together and we came here to talk about the marriage of your son and my brother's daughter" looking at Rajan's father.

Tiwari uncle knew that Rajan loved Tanya more than anything but still, as a matter of confirmation, he asked "Rajan, what do you say?"

The answer was expected. I mean the expression was expected as he didn't open his mouth but everyone understood that he was happy as he nodded with his eyes facing the floor of our room.

Everything went well and good and Rajan's marriage was fixed after his engineering as both of them were not old enough to marry.

Chapter 10

Today

I am going to meet Inchara today. I was asking her to meet from the day she accepted my proposal. Now it's nearly a year and a half and I am very happy that I am going to meet her.

The winner of the last election in Navanagar constituency was BB. There remains only one party now-the party which was formed by the father of Mr Manan and BB. The party leader of it is BB now and Mr. Manan Sharma is the elder advisor for Mr. Karan Sharma.

Recently I went near the Navanagar stadium at 4 in the morning to meet Naseer, I thought that I may not find him as it had been a very long time and even if he comes there he will not recognise me as I met him only once till then. He was there and with some biscuit packets in his hand when I stopped my two wheeler in front of that tea stall.

He recognised me and said "you are better than my son, that day I told you that he would come once in six months to see me but he hadn't come from the day I told you that." "A month back he called me and said he will not be able to come for few months, he is saying the same from the day you met me. That too he does not call every day, not even every week, not even a month maybe three or four months." He said in a crying tone. I hugged him after hearing that and said him that I would be there with him at least once in a week.

I am doing engineering now, Rajan, Punith and Jaffar are doing the same but we all are in different colleges. I am not staying with Rajan as my college is too far from Navanagar and not even have a song of my own with Punith from nearly a year now.

Tanya is pursuing Bachelor's degree in Commerce, Rajan drops her to college everyday either in his bike or in his father's car. Rajan, Tiwari uncle and Sulekha are staying in the house where once BB's family used to stay.

BB and his family are now staying with Karan Sharma's family and they are one of the happiest joint families I have ever seen. To be frank we call or text each other once in a fortnight and meet once in two or three months, things are changed but this story remain the same.

Somehow I found love, but how? where? when?

Chapter 11

Epilogue

After getting to know what all happened, do you think I found love? If yes where did I find love? When and how?

Inchara was not staying in any fifth cross so it was impossible to find love in fifth cross if you think only that is love.

Then what is love? Did I find love in fifth cross?

Yes, I did

Was it the thing which made Christina kiss that guy of motor cycle? No, because he was kissing someone else just after some weeks, maybe a couple of months.

Then what was it?

Was it the thing which Rajan had for Tanya and Tanya had for Rajan? or was it the thing which I had for Inchara and Inchara had for me?

Obviously it was but it was not only the love, I saw or found or experienced during the whole stay at 5th cross.

I found love in that mother who was running behind a moving bus just because her son left the lunch box.

I found love in that old security guard's face who was living only for his grandson.

I found love in the face of that child which got a fish bowl at the same instant of time I found love in the child's father's face as he saw his child happy.

I found love in Naseer towards those dogs and love in those dogs towards Naseer.

I found love in Jaffar towards Rajan when he came back from that annual day function.

To be frank, I found love in that corrupt police officer towards money.

Even I found love in the friends of Sudesh as they were there with him even if they knew that there can be problem to them in future.

It may seem funny if I say to you that you can find love in war. I mean not the war which happens between you and your friend but the war between countries. How? There will be just blood there. Love in war! nothing is there to be amazed, even if the actions from the soldiers are brutal, they are doing it as they love their country.

It is not like there should be a human of your opposite sex to find love, it shows you don't know what love really is. Love can happen to a male and female as the whole world knows or it can be seen everywhere.

Look the world around you, you will surely find love everywhere, in every creature, it may be human or may not be. I have seen love in dogs and even you can find love in any animal.

I, Rahul Ramesh assure you that love is not just a feeling which makes you a man or woman. It is the feeling which makes you a human.